Acting Edition

The Betrothed

by Dipika Guha

SAMUEL FRENCH

No one shall make any changes in this title(s) for the purpose of production. No part of this book may be reproduced, stored in a retrieval system, scanned, uploaded, or transmitted in any form, by any means, now known or yet to be invented, including mechanical, electronic, digital, photocopying, recording, videotaping, or otherwise, without the prior written permission of the publisher. No one shall share this title(s), or any part of this title(s), through any social media or file hosting websites.

For all inquiries regarding motion picture, television, online/digital and other media rights, please contact Concord Theatricals Corp.

MUSIC AND THIRD-PARTY MATERIALS USE NOTE

Licensees are solely responsible for obtaining formal written permission from copyright owners to use copyrighted music and/or other copyrighted third-party materials (e.g. artworks, logos) in the performance of this play and are strongly cautioned to do so. If no such permission is obtained by the licensee, then the licensee must use only original music and materials that the licensee owns and controls. Licensees are solely responsible and liable for clearances of all third-party copyrighted materials, including without limitation music, and shall indemnify the copyright owners of the play(s) and their licensing agent, Concord Theatricals Corp., against any costs, expenses, losses and liabilities arising from the use of such copyrighted third-party materials by licensees. For music, please contact the appropriate music licensing authority in your territory for the rights to any incidental music.

IMPORTANT BILLING AND CREDIT REQUIREMENTS

If you have obtained performance rights to this title, please refer to your licensing agreement for important billing and credit requirements.

THE BETROTHED premiered at Wellfleet Harbor Actors Theatre in Wellfleet, MA on August 4, 2011. The Artistic Director was Jeff Zinn. It was directed by Jesse Jou, with set design by Ted Vitale, costume design by Moria Sine Clinton, lighting design by Bridget Doyle, and sound design & original music by Nathan A. Roberts. The Stage Manager was Alaina Sciascia. The play was subsequently produced at Chester Theatre in Chester, MA on August 15, 2012. The cast was as follows:

SIMON. . . . . Andy Place

CECILIA / RASHEEDA. . . . . Caitlin Clouthier

THE PRIEST / GONAN . . . . John Shuman

SOLOMON / CECIL (SIMON'S SON) . . . . Ron Daniels

This play was written and developed at the Yale School of Drama and owes its life to Paula Vogel and the actors who worked on it; Max Gordon Moore, Alex Henrikson, Babak Tafti and Ben Horner.

CHARACTERS

SIMON – mid-30s, an American man, a virgin, existentially anxious, his favourite movie is *When Harry Met Sally*.

ANNA CECILIA RASHEEDA SILOSA HANGI MARIA – as old as possible for a woman on stage, arises from a dark mythical Eastern European country, has never seen a movie but has lived the life of several.

    ***RASHEEDA ANNA CECILIA SILOSA HANGI MARIA** – mid-30s although insists she is in her early 20s, daughter to Anna Cecilia stunning, a model, does not like movies.

SOLOMON – late-50s, handsome, dirt underneath his fingernails, speaks with an accent of a man from a mythical Eastern European country who has spent his life watching American movies like *Die Hard* and *The Godfather*.

    ***CECIL** – early teens, Simon's son wants to be in the movies someday, a silent part.

GONAN – late-50s, Solomon's best friend and worst enemy, a fan of silent comedies.

    ***THE PRIEST** – late-40s, the local priest, has recently got into watching American teen shows like *90210* and *The Hills*.

*Characters with an asterisk are played by the primary cast: Anna, Solomon and Gonan as a breakdown for doubling.

SETTING

Place

Where the sun and moon are always a perfect circle. Where the night is perfectly black.

Where the mornings are bright hot.

(And the afternoons are even hotter…sleep is necessary or else you might be prone to error when delivering a calf.)

Where, despite the heat, the soil smells freshly rained on.

Where the earth is perfectly round. And you can feel its roundness.

Where one's main occupation is thinking the thought that occurs in the afternoon, just before that sleep.

Locations

An aeroplane

A graveyard

The afterlife

A home

TIME

Present Day

Action of Time

One week

AUTHOR'S NOTES

Extended ellipses look like this '...'
These are not pauses. They indicate that the characters are actively responding, but in silence.

Anna Cecilia Rasheeda's hair is described as black, and curly. The production may change this to whatever color the actor's hair happens to be.

These characters all possess the simplicity and purity of clowns. Every moment is deeply felt and true.

When lying, they believe wholeheartedly in the lie.

They live happily in the state of paradox and contradiction.

Music

Licensees are encouraged to create their own.

The Journey

Sunday Morning

*(A lone aeroplane seat floats in the darkness. **SIMON** sits. He plugs his earphones in. Loud music.* He quickly turns the volume down and shifts uncomfortably in his seat. He slips an airline eyemask over his eyes and clutches a blanket that he discovers only goes up to his knees. He tries to cover himself up, but, in the effort, he only exposes another part of his body. He rips the eyemask off. He talks to the woman in his seat next to him. She's invisible to us.)*

SIMON. Back to the old cow country, back to the old homeland.

*(She presumably responds with a polite smile; **SIMON** takes this as a cue to continue.)*

Don't you just hate it when people you don't know talk to you on the plane? Yakking about their lives, taking up your personal space? I can't stand it. I mean, I love to travel. I just hate leaving home because I really love America. But these days what with these airfares... fly anywhere you want for, like a dollar, right? And everybody has a dollar! So you can just go... *(He gets visibly nervous.)* find out where you came from...who it is you've been waiting your whole life to...

---

* A license to produce *The Betrothed* does not include a performance license for any third-party or copyrighted recordings. Licensees should create their own.

So, hey, listen to me yakking on! You gonna be gone long? You seeing the river and the, the hills and the geysers? Oh, you totally should. I bought this great guidebook. It's got everything we need you know, 'cause us Americans...boy they see us coming! We gotta stick together in these places. So, if you need anything, feel free to...here...take my card *(He digs out a card from his jacket.)*. It's my first time. Flying, I mean, flying, it's my first... I've been to first base, I mean, domestic, I mean domestic bases uh airport bases, uhm but this is my first time over this body of of...water.

(He's dug his own grave, he presses on.)

I've been watching *Sex and the City*. Those girls! They just fly all over the place. I can see why you women like it. It's, like really, really, the women are really, I mean, women are really...anyway...my Mom always said women would take over the world and look at you now, I mean, not *you*, I mean not you personally, but you know I can't help feeling that the guys on these shows are uh... (have you seen them?) they're really...because how many men are...like *that*... My Mom always...you know she really worries...about me finding...someone so I'm... I'm...

Awwww. Are you asleep? You look so sweet.

(She's most definitely faking sleep.)

That's okay, you sleep. I'll be fine, because it's my first time with, but everyone has a first time, right?

(He inhales deeply. Then quietly, to himself.)

Back to the old cow country Simon...back to the old homeland.

(Slow half-light. Roar of an aeroplane that sounds like it's both taking off and landing at

*the same time. The shadow of a plane passes
behind* **SIMON** *and then seeps into his body.)*

*(He watches the shadow leak into his skin
and then releases it through the open palm of
his hand.)*

*(Lights fade and rise with uplifting Eastern
European wedding music.*)*

---

* A license to produce *The Betrothed* does not include a performance
license for any third-party or copyrighted music. Licensees should create
an original composition or use music in the public domain. For further
information, please see the Music and Third-Party Materials Use Note
on page iii.

The Test

Sunday Afternoon

(**SIMON** *stands outside a door. Visible inside is a rickety table, three chairs, a fold-up bed and a tinny transistor radio [where the music now leaks out from].* The table has two plates, three mugs and a pack of cards. A second door leads outside. An empty mouse cage sits by the door.)*

(A window or a window frame with shutters hangs upstage for easy passage of day and night.)

(A pile of ragged men's shoes lies in one corner of the room. There is hay on the floor.)

(Inside, a hunched-over **CECILIA** *in black sways gently to herself. The hunched figure rises.)*

(She hobbles over to the doorway.)

(She holds her age in every limb, in every pore of her body, every crease in her face, every strand of her hair. It is as though time folded in on itself.)

(She flings open the door. They talk over the music.)

SIMON. I've come for my wife!

CECILIA. She's dead.

---

* A license to produce *The Betrothed* does not include a performance license for any third-party or copyrighted recordings. Licensees should create their own.

(The music grinds to a halt.)

SIMON. …

CECILIA. …

SIMON. What? No? Is she inside?

CECILIA. No.

Because she's dead.

SIMON. Where is everyone?

CECILIA. They came for the funeral.

Then the sun came out, so they went for a picnic. They left their shoes.

(She points to a pile of men's shoes heaped in a corner of the room.)

SIMON. But… I flew all this way, I flew! I hate flying. They take your shoes away; they throw away your toothpaste. Strangers talk to you the whole time, it's terrible. All for what? I was going to be married TODAY. Today! Why did this happen to me?

CECILIA. I don't know. I don't know you.

SIMON. My father.

CECILIA. And her father.

SIMON. Made a pact. They betrothed their most beloved to their most beloved.

CECILIA. Your father.

SIMON. And her father.

CECILIA. Lost a bet. You won Gonan's ugliest daughter.

Lucky for you Gonan had no ugly daughters.

So, you got the smallest.

She was perfect, except for one extra finger on her left foot.

SIMON. Toe?

CECILIA. Finger.

But she's gone now.

SIMON. Dead?

CECILIA. Dead.

She was like a daughter to me.

SIMON. Rasheeda, my wife!

CECILIA. Rasheeda?

SIMON. My wife!

CECILIA. …

There appears to be a mix up.

SIMON. She's not dead?

CECILIA. Oh no Rasheeda's not dead.

SIMON. What? So where is she?

CECILIA. I thought you meant the one who did die…

Ramida. Ramida died.

From warts.

Rasheeda's not dead.

She's out back with the cows.

SIMON. Is this the ugly one?

CECILIA. This *is* the ugly one. Here I was thinking "I wonder why Gonan offloaded the nice looking one with the extra finger?" Then I thought, the extra finger is useful for scrubbing those bits behind the toilet, so you see I was confused, but no reason, because the ugly one's right here, in the back. Waiting for you…

SIMON. Scrubbing the cows…

CECILIA. Or scrubbing herself. I can't tell, their behinds are so alike. I'll go fetch her.

SIMON. No, don't.

CECILIA. Then leave.

SIMON. If I leave, she'll think I'm a coward.

CECILIA. At least you won't be a married coward.

SIMON. She's waiting?

CECILIA. Waiting, washing, waiting…

SIMON. All those years.

CECILIA. Betrothed their most beloved to their most beloved.

SIMON. Waiting for me.

CECILIA. That's all she does. Wait.

Nowhere to go. Nothing to be.

Even when she wants to go far, far away.

To follow her dream.

Nowhere to go Nowhere to be.

Except, maybe, next to her beloved.

SIMON. Me?

But I didn't know what it would be like!

CECILIA. Like?

SIMON. Like!

CECILIA. You're a man, what's not to like?

SIMON. She'll understand if I go…

CECILIA. Go! Because once you give your word to a woman, living or dead, there's no turning back.

Especially if you were

CECILIA.	**SIMON.**
Betrothed.	Betrothed.

CECILIA. It's sacred.

Deadly.

Run! Save yourself!

>(**SIMON** *turns to run out. He stops.*)

SIMON. My father and her father played cards back in the days when men were men. All I want is to lie under the covers and breathe. Breathe my father's breaths. To know where I belong. So, if this, if this is what it means to know my place, I'll, I'll stay.

>(**CECILIA** *stares at him and then turns quickly.*)

>(*She exits out of the back door.* **SIMON** *waits. He sees the deck of cards on the table and pulls one from the pack. It is the Joker. He returns it hastily.*)

>(*A small cough at the door. He turns.*)

>(**CECILIA** *walks in again wearing a wedding dress.*)

CECILIA. I am Rasheeda...your wife. This is *my* house.

Seduction of the Tongue

Sunday Evening

(**SIMON** *and* **CECILIA** *sit at the table together.* **SIMON** *looks dumbstruck.* **CECILIA** *pours coffee.*)

CECILIA. Did you look outside Simon? How green the garden looks against the mountain gone dry from the happiness of summer. In winter he weeps, and the garden does not look as green. And the tree outside? She waits for me every day when I come home from my afternoon swim. I smell of the lake, the tree bends down to smell the nape of my neck. I dry in the heat of the sun.

SIMON. That's great.

CECILIA. Your English is weak.

Where did you learn it?

SIMON. Pittsburgh.

CECILIA. Don't worry, we'll return your language to you, Simon son of Simon.

You're as skinny as a rake. Just like your father.

SIMON. My father?

CECILIA. Your father was a rake who had all the girls; pretty girls, ugly girls, toothy girls, hairy girls, girls who existed, girls who didn't.

SIMON. What *is* this?

CECILIA. Your father once stole a girl from his brother's dreams. In that dream, his brother was sitting in a library reading a book, when in walked the most stop-your-heart beautiful woman. Now this library had tall ceilings and windows and enough books to build a house with.

Perfect for fucking.

So, this woman comes in and without any courtship, they began to do their business. So, they meet like this, every night, and then one night, the woman stops coming. Just like that, no warning, no sign. Nothing.

So that morning, your uncle comes down for breakfast looking like he dropped his heart down a well.

And your father, he's there, drinking his coffee. He says, "What's the matter brother, you look terrible" and back comes the reply, "You know brother, I have this dream every night this beautiful woman comes to me. We make love until I wake. I wake with her sound inside my skin. Last night she didn't come." So, your father asks, "Does she have dark hair on her upper arms, big eyelashes and a squint?" And your uncle replies "Yes, she's beautiful."

And your father says, "She's with me now." So that's the kind of man he was.

Long arms to steal women. Long everything...

Or so we heard.

SIMON. Okay. This is just like that movie where the couple don't meet until right at the very end. Only, we're at the beginning (even if it looks like the end for you.)

I never met my wife, but I know she doesn't look like you.

You're not the one Rasheeda.

CECILIA. I am the one.

SIMON. How old are you?

CECILIA. Thirty-two.

I only look like this because of age. You look as old as you feel.

And I feel. Like this. Old.

You should have come yesterday, Simon son of Simon, I was really good looking then.

Then I aged. It was sudden. Suddenly.

The world.

It turned round.

I saw one half of it was green, the other brown.

Half of the world in darkness while the other half in light. Only half of us have food to eat, the other half have nothing.

And some people fly halfway around the world to get something.

They cannot see

That there is no prize to get.

Then I felt this sadness, deep inside my life, I tapped a dark well of grief.

I sat under the tree outside and cried these tears that wet the earth. And then when I came back into the house and looked in the mirror.

I saw my face had aged. My hair had whitened. I became as you see me now.

Forever changed.

And then I remembered you were coming, and I thought "Nevermind, these things happen."

SIMON. Okay. So, where I come from, you have to be able to, to look at your wife. To take her to office parties or, or, Halloween parties. You have to be able to take her out. Side.

Where I come from Rasheeda. What your wife looks like. It matters.

CECILIA. The arch of her back, the strength in the soles of her feet, the dance her heart makes.

It all matters...

I love myself Simon son of Simon. How many women love themselves?

SIMON. *(Trying again.)* Okay. So, *this* is what it's like. It's like online shopping. You order something because the description looks great and even though there's no picture you order it anyway, and then it comes through in the mail except...

CECILIA. *(Interrupting him.)* You are a very handsome man...

SIMON. Okay! So this is what I want! I want to meet a woman in a railway carriage. She's sitting alone. A book falls on her head. She looks up. She sees me, I smile. It's my book. I don't want it to be heavy. I want it to be serious, but not heavy like a dictionary. I don't want to kill her. Just slight concussion so I can hold her.

CECILIA. I'm so happy Simon son of Simon, can you tell?

SIMON. No.

CECILIA. What if I do this with my mouth?

SIMON. No...

CECILIA. This?

SIMON. No!

CECILIA. It'll get better. That's the way marriages work, they get better with time, when the passion fades...

SIMON. WHAT passion?!

CECILIA. How sweet it is not to have to work so hard for love. To do nothing but wait with patience. Every fibre of your body active, humming quietly...like your aeroplane.

SIMON. *(Realizing.)* There was no profile picture online.

Rasheeda, why was there no profile picture online???

CECILIA. My father he had all these issues. Depression, fibromyalgia. All these invisible problems.

So, when he heard about the internet it scared him right down to his grave.

We were getting ready for the funeral when we heard you were coming.

Too late for a profile picture.

SIMON. Were you afraid?

That if I saw what you look like, I might not come?

CECILIA. You would have come.

Everyone comes for their betrothed.

SIMON. People marry for love.

CECILIA. Not when they are betrothed!

When betrothed people marry, they know more than other people. When they close their eyes together in the dark, they become more compassionate, the wealth comes together, it's good for the environment.

Look outside, you have been here now one hour according to the cock.

SIMON. Clock?

CECILIA. Cock. He'll crow again in a minute.

(*A cock crows.*)

You see animals?

Always licking each other?

What would they do if they had no one to lick?

SIMON. What would they do?

CECILIA. They'd lick themselves.

Is this the behavior for a human being? The cock lives here Simon.

With me!

Tomorrow we'll bring the rabbits and hens to bed with us, okay?

They like to play, it's fun! We can play house in the sheets, you can show me what it's like to be cold in Pittsburgh. You can hold me like it is in the wintertime.

SIMON. This has been very nice Rasheeda, but I have to go now

CECILIA. *(Interrupting him.)* Ahh...listen...can you hear them? All the women out there.

In the starless skies.

In the sealess shores. In the tallest buildings. They all harbor longing.

Unspeakable longing for their betrothed.

SIMON. I... I flew here on a plane.

A plane with hard edges and soft seats.

I saw the hard nose of the plane flying straight into a heart. A heart good and pure.

A lap soft and sweet.

I never talk like this, my tongue feels loose...my head feels soft... What is this?

> *(Drowsy,* **SIMON** *lies down on the bed.* **CECILIA** *closes the window.)*

CECILIA. Some men wait their whole life to find their place. And you have found it.

Here. With me. Take your shoes off Simon son of Simon. Give them to me.

You do not feel it yet.

But this is going *very* well

(**SIMON** *curls up on the fold-up bed.* **CECILIA** *tosses his shoes onto the pile of men's shoes. She reaches inside her clothes. She pulls out a pair of rings. She puts one ring on his finger and one on her own. She puts on her wedding veil and slips outside into the moonlight.*)

(*Outside,* **CECILIA** *sings.*)

[CECILIA'S SONG: "CECILIA SINGS A SONG IN PRAISE OF HER OWN BEAUTY"]

STRIP THE MOUNTAIN BARE, UNDERNEATH
THE RIVER DIES.
STRIP THE OCEANS COLD, UNDERNEATH
THE EARTH CRIES.
FOLLOWING THE HIDDEN SIGNS
SO MANY TIMES,
LOVE'S PASSED ME BY.
NONE COULD SEE ME, UNDERNEATH.

STRIP THE CLOUDS OF RAIN, UNDERNEATH
THE PEOPLE SIGH.
STRIP THE HOUSES CLEAN, UNDERNEATH
THE HOME SURVIVES.
FOLLOWING THE SECRET SIGNS
SO MANY TIMES,
LOVE'S PASSED ME BY.
NONE COULD SEE ME, UNDERNEATH.

NOW I'VE SPOKEN TO THE MOUNTAIN
SUNG TO THE EARTH. ARGUED WITH THE TREES,
   CONVINCED THEM OF MY WORTH

OF HOW I'M BEAUTIFUL. I'M FUCKING BEAUTIFUL.
I KNOW THIS NOW THE EARTH'S DONE ITS (DUTIFUL)
   RETURN
SO MANY TIMES, THAT I'M MORE BEAUTIFUL
I'M IMMUTABLE. STRIPPED OF MY VANITY, I CAN TRULY
   BE.

STRIP ME OF MY BONES, UNDERNEATH
MY SOUL SHINES.
STRIP MY HAIR OF CURLS, UNDERNEATH
MY BALDNESS THRIVES.
FOLLOWING LOVE'S LITTLE SIGNS
SO MANY TIMES,
I'VE WEPT AND CRIED
FOR SOMEONE TO SEE ME, UNDERNEATH

OF HOW I'M BEAUTIFUL. I'M FUCKING BEAUTIFUL.
I KNOW THIS NOW THE EARTH'S DONE ITS (DUTIFUL)
    RETURN
SO MANY TIMES
THAT I'M MORE BEAUTIFUL
I'M IMMUTABLE.
STRIPPED OF MY VANITY I CAN TRULY *BE*.
I'M BEAUTIFUL.
SO FUCKING BEAUTIFUL. BRIGHTER THAN BRIGHT STARS
WHO DON'T KNOW WHO THEY ARE.
CLEARER THAN THE RING
SOME POOR GUY HAD TO SPRING.

IT'S TIME FOR THE RECKONING.

OF JUST HOW BEAUTIFUL, IN FACT, I'VE ALWAYS BEEN.

    (She speaks.)

Sleep Simon sleep...because you won't get much more
of that this week!

    *(She runs inside as fast as she can and leaps
    into bed.)*

Seduction of the Mouth

Sunday Night

(Cecilia's wedding dress lies on the floor laid to waste in haste. She sits on the bed wearing something she believes is lingerie. Moonlight streams in from the open window. **SIMON** *lies in bed, he is just waking.)*

CECILIA. The first time I was wed, I was flung on the back of a cart. Like an ear of corn. Raw, wet with rain. Then my husband came and threw me over his shoulder. I hated the moon and the stars and the trees. I hated the world for giving me to a man with no feeling in his heart. But that man was not my betrothed…

*(***SIMON*** sits up suddenly in bed.)*

SIMON. Where am I?

CECILIA. Come home Simon son of Simon. Be a witness to my breasts, one at a time or both at once if you choose…

SIMON. I don't want to.

CECILIA. You're American, all you do is want!

SIMON. Okay. So, where I come from you have to be able to, to take your wife to office parties and Halloween parties. You have to be able to take her out. Side. Where I come from Rasheeda…

CECILIA. Let me hold you with my gums Simon son of Simon.

SIMON. Oh God.

CECILIA. No God will stop me from being with you, feeling you touch every part of my body.

The secret parts and the loud parts, the loving parts and the cool parts, which, I have to tell you, grow warm with the thought of you…

SIMON. I can't do this.

(She puts her hands on her own face.)

CECILIA. You aged me even more with your complaining. "I don't want to marry an old woman, I don't want to marry an old woman…!" Some people, they don't have wives. Can you imagine?

SIMON. I didn't have a wife. I was fine!

CECILIA. You were not fine.

You were like a lonely cheetah without a friend to lick.

Now you have a friend to lick.

Your father…

SIMON. My father?

CECILIA. Played cards.

SIMON. Back in the days when men were men.

CECILIA. The women…

SIMON. What women?

CECILIA. Came to him stacked –

Like cards.

He did not have to chase love.

Close your eyes Simon son of Simon let me lead you around our marriage bed, now dry but soon wet with the humble juices of our betrothal.

SIMON. Stay where you are.

CECILIA. You must stop Simon. You must *be*. Or else you will see nothing.

Feel nothing.

SIMON. Stop.

CECILIA. I asked you nicely, very nicely to move into bed. To rest your head.

To behave nice to your wife.

YOU DID NOT HAVE TO TAKE ME.

SIMON. BUT I DID!

CECILIA. BUT YOU DID!

SIMON. I HAD NOT SEEN YOUR FACE!

Please! Rasheeda. I am disappointed. With my life.

My father, he always said I would amount to nothing.

Today was going to change everything. I was going to marry.

My betrothed would save me, would give me somewhere to, to be.

The love of my life in the firmament that always was, always is and always will be.

CECILIA. I don't know about the firmament, but I know how things work under the sheets.

SIMON. That's inappropriate Rasheeda for a woman of your age!

CECILIA. Let me seduce you Simon son of Simon!

SIMON. I want to be with a woman who isn't so old that you can still tell that she's a woman.

CECILIA. Your father was seventy-six when he died and he was still a man.

SIMON. Yes, he was, always a man and I can't even sleep with a real woman. Look at me! I've got nothing but a dream of a woman I want to worship, whose feet I want to kiss, whose body I want to raise up to the stars.

CECILIA. Put your face between my legs Simon son of Simon!

SIMON. Get away from me!

CECILIA. Let me eat you. Let me tear into your flesh with my gums.

Let me hold you in my mouth without danger to you.

SIMON. Don't touch me!

CECILIA. Try! You'll like.

> *(Lights go out suddenly.* **CECILIA** *shows* **SIMON** *something. And then a little more. And then a little more. Pitch black. Their cries split the night. Moments pass.)*

What did you think of that?

SIMON. *(Blown away.)* Oh...oh my god, oh Rasheeda I...

CECILIA. Let me tell you a story.

Once upon a time there was a young man with a huge...

SIMON. Stop!

CECILIA. And he came all the way from America to find his beloved because in America all the women were too boring and too busy, and it is cold so you can't live without your shoes.

So, he came all this way for one woman.

Just one.

With large eyes like unpolluted lakes. Where the fish still have two eyes and the turtles four feet.

Simon?

> *(***SIMON*** *lies on the bed, blissfully exhausted. Lights go up.)*

SIMON. Oh my God, it's still you!

CECILIA. Who else?

SIMON. You did that...to me?

CECILIA. Do you have a fever?

SIMON. What have I done?

CECILIA. Was my desire too pure?

I love you.

SIMON. You're too old for love.

You're deluded.

CECILIA. Pointless passion?

SIMON. Totally!

CECILIA. Then let's do it again and again and again!

SIMON. Stop. Wait!

No, stop! Let's...play a game.

CECILIA. OOH.

What shall we play?

SIMON. Let's play...put a sack on your face? Do you know that one?

CECILIA. No but I like sacks...

SIMON. Will you wear one for me?

CECILIA. I could wear a sack, Simon.

SIMON. Would you?

CECILIA. Wait here, I'll go get it.

> (*She hobbles out.* **SIMON** *looks around, frantic. He begins to pick up his things to make a quick exit.*)

> (*As he's about to leave,* **CECILIA** *reenters wearing a sack over her head. She waddles in, bumping straight into every wall.* **SIMON** *skirts away from her grasp. She follows blindly, relentlessly.*)

CECILIA. Is it better like this?

SIMON. Much better Rasheeda.

CECILIA. Do you like me like this?

SIMON. Yes, very much!

CECILIA. Is this a game? I love games.

SIMON. Me too, Rasheeda I love games too!

CECILIA. You want me to pose? You want me to say some words Simon son of Simon?

SIMON. You can just stand there.

(**CECILIA** *stands expectantly, sack over her head.*)

CECILIA. What happens now?

SIMON. I don't know! Why don't you lie down Rasheeda?

CECILIA. But I'm not tired. Let's begin the game.

SIMON. Begin!

CECILIA. BEGIN!

SIMON. …

CECILIA. …

(*She stands.*)

This can't be all…why don't I come to you?

(*She makes a leap for the bed and falls flat on her face.* **SIMON** *freezes.* **CECILIA** *lies stock still.*)

Don't worry I'm not dead!

(**SIMON** *watches as she waddles haphazardly around the room, concussed. She finally swivels and pinpoints in the direction of the* *bed. She leans over to the bed and reaches out to be kissed.)*

*(**SIMON** reaches out for her as though to kiss her. His hands find his way to **CECILIA**'s neck. He grips tightly and squeezes.)*

(Blackout.)

Deathly Error

Monday Afternoon

(Funeral music. **SIMON** and the **PRIEST** stand at Cecilia's grave. **SIMON** finds that he is still holding the sack. He hides it around his back. Bright sun. A pair of binoculars hangs around the **PRIEST**'s neck. He wipes his brow.)*

PRIEST. We gather here to celebrate the life of Anna Cecilia...

SIMON. Who?

PRIEST. Rasheeda Anna Cecilia.

SIMON. Oh.

PRIEST. Silosa-Hangi-Maria.

SIMON. I never knew her full name.

PRIEST. Married.

SIMON. What?

PRIEST. Never.

Divorced...

SIMON. When?

PRIEST. Never.

Evil.

SIMON. I know right!

---

* A license to produce *The Betrothed* does not include a performance license for any third-party or copyrighted music. Licensees should create an original composition or use music in the public domain. For further information, please see the Music and Third-Party Materials Use Note on page iii.

PRIEST. Never!

The best woman in the town, laid to rest like this on a Monday. Dear ones. It is natural when the betrothed of a young woman comes home, we should not see her for a while. We were not to know however, that she was to vanish from our lives forever.

The last time I saw Anna Cecilia.

SIMON. Rasheeda.

PRIEST. Rasheeda Anna Cecilia.

I was watching with my binoculars. Looking to see the big red sun. Instead, I saw a big red

SIMON. Stop!

PRIEST. On her front lawn, ripe in her thirty-two years. In the midday sun, without a care in the world awaiting her beloved.

Her long

SIMON. White.

PRIEST. Black.

Hair cascading over her shoulders. Like rain. Her skin.

SIMON. Rough.

PRIEST. Smooth against the rough grass...

In the hot summer light, I was blinded by what I believed was the sun.

But I later realized, it was nothing but her beauty.

Anna Cecilia.

SIMON. Rasheeda?!

PRIEST. Rasheeda Anna Cecilia awaited her beloved's arrival.

And today he stands with us. Mourning the woman, he travelled thousands of miles away from his own life and work, to be with.

One of our best women in this town was to be his wife, his companion of many days and just as many nights.

He was to look after her. Cherish her.

Kiss her feet.

Raise her to the stars.

But now the most we can do is remember her beauty.

The way it was on a Saturday early afternoon/late evening. And think on the marvelous woman who was Anna Cecilia.

SIMON. Rasheeda.

PRIEST. Rasheeda Anna Cecilia Silosa Hangi Maria!

Let me take this moment to confess to you.

All night the men in this town would dream of you. You could feel all the dreams rising in the night.

All the dreams in a giant cloud.

And then it would rain in the morning. Small warm droplets from the sky.

You'd feed the crops; you'd touch the skin of the men as they left to work. We'd breathe you in.

Divine precipitation. Amen.

> (**SIMON** *looks at the* **PRIEST** *in amazement.*)

SIMON. Amen.

PRIEST. What will you do now my son?

SIMON. Father, I've come all this way. It seems a shame to spend all my time at a funeral.

It might be good to harness my grief. Take solace in newfound (platonic) friendships?

It might be good to see some other young, fresh... female faces. Do you know any Father?

PRIEST. There are, indeed, other faces.

But alas, the face of your betrothed is like no other. She was special.

Now she is lost.

SIMON. Desperately lost.

PRIEST. I feel for you.

Left your home, your phones, your wireless internet connection, all for what? To meet your beloved, the one you were betrothed to from birth.

SIMON. Actually, I was five.

My father lost a game of gin rummy.

PRIEST. All this bright happy expectation to be met by death. Death the opposite of life.

Go to the bars now. Cultivate what good you can from this terrible time. Go and drink for her.

She had no family anymore you know. Your father was like a father to her.

Visiting her, taking her food when she was ill.

SIMON. My father? Would visit her?

PRIEST. He'd visit every day almost at one point if I remember correctly. Always carrying little remembrances, little gifts.

SIMON. My father? With presents? And then?

PRIEST. Death.

SIMON. Yes...death.

PRIEST. So, she stopped leaving the house. I'd look sometimes.

And then I'd see her.

Legs long enough to straddle the mountains between us.

SIMON. Father!

PRIEST. I can see we do not know each other well enough yet. I knew your father.

Take my card.

(He hands **SIMON** *a playing card.)*

PRIEST. Let's take time to get to know each other's neuroses. The American way.

You know at times like this, it's common for people to ask themselves "Why?" or "Why me?"

SIMON. Why would I do that?

PRIEST. Why? Oh well, sometimes when a tragedy like this happens, people tend to assume that there is something wrong with them. That they are in some way the cause, I wanted to come and tell you that, that is not at all the case.

SIMON. I am the cause.

PRIEST. No, you're not.

SIMON. Yes, yes I am.

I DID IT.

I made this happen…

I have to tell you the truth! When I walked in…

Father, she was.

Old.

PRIEST. Mature.

SIMON. Old! Like a…

Like a hat with holes.

She was holey.

PRIEST. Sacred.

SIMON. No.

She was.

…ugly. Like a sack.

PRIEST. Of flowers?

SIMON. No.

PRIEST. Of sunshine?

SIMON. No!

PRIEST. Perhaps where you come from, all the women have shining skin and eyes as clear as unpolluted water?

But Rasheeda Anna Cecilia.

Was a rarity in these parts.

Here look I kept a photograph from Saturday.

SIMON. No, thank you Father. I've seen enough.

PRIEST. It's little but a ghost of her memory, have a glance.

(He pulls a photograph from his clothes. **SIMON** *can't help but look.)*

SIMON. Who is this?!

PRIEST. Anna Cecilia.

SIMON. Then who's in the ground?

PRIEST. Rasheeda Anna Cecilia Silosa Hangi Maria

SIMON. From when?

PRIEST. Saturday late afternoon/early evening.

SIMON. What have I done? She was telling the truth! She was beautiful on Saturday

PRIEST. Nothing! I'm trying to tell you, you did nothing!

SIMON. We have to get her back. I have to see my father.

PRIEST. He's dead.

SIMON. It doesn't matter.

PRIEST. Okay. I'll take you.

My Father (Not my Friend)

Tuesday Morning

(Music.)*

(Two dead men play cards on a park bench. Unless actively interrupted, the game never stops. **SOLOMON** *looks over the cards. He looks at* **GONAN**. *He drops a card with great force.* **GONAN** *jumps. Trembling, he puts down a card.)*

*(***SIMON** *enters. He looks between the two men, unsure.)*

SOLOMON. Who do you think you are Gonan, you dead sack of shit.

*(***SOLOMON** *sees* **SIMON**. *A glimmer in his eye. He quickly returns to the cards.)*

Deadwood.

(To **GONAN**.*)* Don't think you can undercut this you bastard. Gin. Game. I win.

SIMON. You're still playing...

SOLOMON. ...

GONAN. ...

SIMON. Mind if I join you? I don't mean to disturb you... I could just sit right here...

---

* A license to produce *The Betrothed* does not include a performance license for any third-party or copyrighted music. Licensees should create an original composition or use music in the public domain. For further information, please see the Music and Third-Party Materials Use Note on page iii.

(**SIMON** *creeps towards the bench. The men continue to play.*)

Right here on the edge, you'd hardly notice me

(*The men don't make space.*)

Or...not. Standing is just as good.

Dad there's something I need to talk to you about.

I need your advice. Dad?

Hey...look how good at cards you are...

SOLOMON. No shit, you stop playing you die.

SIMON. I'd talk to Ma about this, but she can't hear so well.

SOLOMON. That's why I left. Woman was a mouth.

Words were like breath to her.

Keeping her quiet was like drowning a fish. Gin.

(**SOLOMON** *plays, he cheats with a card from his shoe to make a flush.* **GONAN** *notices but says nothing.*)

SIMON. She still thinks about you.

SOLOMON. I was a great lover.

Come into the house real quiet, through the window, get under the kitchen table and under their skirts, tongue first, that's the way to do it.

I was a great lover.

I was a great card player too hah, Gonan?

GONAN. ...

SOLOMON. You lose your hoo ha yet?

SIMON. My what?

SOLOMON. I said your HOO HA?

SIMON. I...

SOLOMON. You're cracking the universe up. My dead spleen just burst.

SIMON. Look, I have to talk to you.

SOLOMON. Isn't that what he's doing Gonan? Talking?

GONAN. ...

SIMON. It's about a woman.

SOLOMON. Women.

Poorer they are the clearer they think. They know what they want.

Me.

You hold your cards that way I can see them Gonan.

Women. They got these eyes like round polluted lakes- where turtles have two feet and the fish four eyes, so don't you swim too long in there huh, Gonan?

Or you'll catch your death hah!

GONAN. ...

SIMON. The woman you betrothed me to.

(**GONAN** *reluctantly parts with a card.*)

SOLOMON. Gonan's kid.

(**GONAN** *nods.*)

SIMON. She's dead.

SOLOMON. No she's not.

SIMON. Yes she is.

SOLOMON. No she's not. I'd know 'cause I'd see her around.

SIMON. I know because I... I killed her.

SOLOMON. You crazy piece of shit from my ass! That's no way to treat a woman. You get her into bed, do the best work you've ever done, then you leave. Where's the death in that?

There's no death!

Gonan, this man is not my son.

Is this the girl I picked out for you?

SIMON. I'm your only son. You picked once!

SOLOMON. Aah, I remember her now. She was a good one...had all her parts. So why did you kill her?

SIMON. I couldn't live with her.

SOLOMON. What? Was she ugly?

SIMON. Yes!

SOLOMON. Oh...

GONAN. (*Apologetic.*) ...

SIMON. She looked like she'd had a bad hair day all over her body.

SOLOMON. You were rash.

Sometimes, if one of their parts stop working...another part will do the job, right Gonan? Lemme explain. So if down there it's all, you know how it gets, and you're having trouble...concentrating your energies, you look at her mouth and you ask yourself "What can I do with that?"

And the answer will surprise you.

The young ones Gonan, too quick to write a woman off. Every cloud has a golden shower.

SIMON. Thing is...

SOLOMON. Just like his mother! Always talking from his mouth. Real men we don't need to talk with our mouths.

We have other parts that do the talking. You understand?

You use your mouth like a woman, you'll turn into one you want that? Right Gonan?

GONAN. …

SIMON. I have to get her back!

You can fix this. You know how things work here.

SOLOMON. Find another woman. One who's not dead. There are others.

SIMON. Well then why did you betroth me to her?

SOLOMON. She was available.

Also, I had gas. From my lunch. These things happen.

Just find another one.

There are some by the donkey shed near Gonan's house.

Or you can use a newspaper, there are pictures in some, right Gonan?

GONAN. …

SOLOMON. Sometimes we buy them to look at the pictures. You can see all the parts. In colour.

SIMON. I've loved this woman my whole life, I need her back.

SOLOMON. Wait for someone to deal you your hand, you'll be waiting forever.

SIMON. What does that mean?

SOLOMON. It means you lose at cards you lose at life.

… Right Gonan?

And there's only one winner…

GONAN. …

(**SOLOMON** *lays down a flush.*)

SOLOMON. Gin.

I win.

Death in the Afternoon

Tuesday Afternoon

(The shutters are closed. It is the dark of a room that has closed bright afternoon light out. **ANNA CECILIA RASHEEDA** *and* **SIMON** *are in deep conversation. They drink coffee.)*

SIMON. I saw the photograph of you Anna Cecilia Rasheeda. The priest who did your funeral, he showed me. You were beautiful.

CECILIA. I was trying to tell you; I am actually very beautiful.

SIMON. I made a terrible mistake.

CECILIA. You were looking too much, too hard, the surface cannot take so much pressure, it's only a surface.

SIMON. I'm so sorry.

CECILIA. It's too bad because I'm dead.

SIMON. All my life I've wanted a wife. A real wife. Who I could have a place with. Next to.

CECILIA. I could have done that for you. But then you killed me.

SIMON. I'm very sorry for killing you.

For making you experience stress.

At your funeral yesterday I looked out into the hills, and I realised how I had come to have certain expectations from my life. My wife, was, up until that time invisible to me too. She lived only in my thoughts,

My dreams, the corners of my bed held you tight in my mind while I slept.

You had habits.

You didn't like to get sand in your shoes. You didn't like to think about snow because it made you feel cold. You could sing ancient songs.

CECILIA. I KNOW ANCIENT SONGS! I can teach you!

You are beginning to learn English Simon.

You feel your mother's tongue in your mouth. Am I your first teacher?

SIMON. Yes...you were lovely.

CECILIA. I am lovely.

SIMON. Will you be my mother?

CECILIA. No.

SIMON. Alright, don't!

But now you've gone and left this gaping hole in my heart, in my life. Thank you for coming back to me... holy woman.

CECILIA. Oh Simon...

I have to go now. I have to go take my place.

(**CECILIA** *stands up to leave.*)

Your father was a good man...

SIMON. My father...

(**CECILIA** *leaves.* **SIMON** *sits. Alone. He thinks.*)

My father...wait, oh no, wait, oh God, don't go to him! Don't do it Rasheeda!

(*A stunningly beautiful young woman,* **RASHEEDA**, *dressed in mourning clothes enters without knocking. She stares at* **SIMON**.)

Who are you?

RASHEEDA. I am Rasheeda. This is *my* house.

[PRIEST'S SONG: "KILLING THE ONES YOU LOVE".]

PRIEST.
IF I DIDN'T HAVE YOU GOD. I WOULD'VE LOST MY WAY
AMONG THE MANY BOYS AND GIRLS WHO NEVER WOULD
    HAVE STAYED.
IF I DIDN'T HAVE YOU GOD, I'D'VE LIVED A LIFE OF SIN
AND SEXY HAPPENINGS
BUT
NOW I HAVE TO DO IT
I HAVE TO SEE IT THROUGH
I CAN'T BE ALWAYS GUIDED BY A LOVE FOR YOU
IF I KILL YOU NOW, IT'LL BE A START. OF AN ETERNAL PATH
AS MY YEARNING QUIET LOVE. MAKES NO SENSE TO YOU
    ABOVE. YOU DON'T SEEM TO WANT MY LOVE
YOU DON'T WANT MY LOVE ...
YOU DON'T WANT MY LOVE!
SO PERHAPS I NEED TO END IT NOW
THE TWO OF US SHOULD PART SOMEHOW ...
LET IT BE KNOWN!
FOR ALL TO MOURN
TODAY'S THE DAY
I KILLED MY GOD. I DID IT QUICK
I TOOK MY STICK
I STUCK YOU GOOD. I KNEW I SHOULD
I KNEW I COULD
A RAPID PROD. HE'S A FRAUD. YOU'RE A FRAUD
I KILLED YOU DEAD I KILLED YOU DEAD

(He stops...)

I SUPPOSE
A ROSE IS A ROSE IS A ROSE... I'VE KILLED YOU DEAD

WHY DOES IT STILL FEEL LIKE YOU'VE WON? I'VE KILLED
   YOU DEAD
BUT IT FEELS LIKE... I'VE KILLED MY SON.

Killing the Ones You Love II

Tuesday Evening

(**SIMON** *and* **RASHEEDA** *are now deep in conversation. They drink coffee.*)

SIMON. So, that's how I killed your mother.

RASHEEDA. But she shouldn't have pretended to be me.

SIMON. That's right. She shouldn't have.

I saw the photograph of you Anna Cecilia Rasheeda.

RASHEEDA. Rasheeda Anna Cecilia.

SIMON. Rasheeda Anna Cecilia.

The priest who did your mother's funeral, he showed it to me. You're beautiful. You look like a model, has anyone ever told you that?

RASHEEDA. That's because I am a model. But only in Europe.

SIMON. Why only in Europe?

RASHEEDA. We all have our limits. The Ural Mountains. That is my boundary.

SIMON. You went to school here?

RASHEEDA. Only until I was eleven.

Then I stopped because I knew everything. Education ruins a person.

Takes away everything they know.

I told my father he quite agreed.

SIMON. He agreed with a ten-year-old who didn't want to go to school?

RASHEEDA. Do you think I'm stupid?

Do you think I'm stupid because I am beautiful?

Beauty arises once, in childhood, like a flower. If it is stopped, the flower will wither. Take students, their flowers have withered.

Their fruit.

Is dead.

SIMON. Two days ago, I was an unmarried man.

Yesterday I was married. And by the evening, I was a murderer. Today, I became a widower. So now I am a widower and a murderer. Tomorrow I would like to be married again.

To you.

Life is full of change.

RASHEEDA. That's the one true thing you've said.

SIMON. Rasheeda.

Will you marry me?

I think it is fated. I killed your only competition (your mother) but in my defense, I based my actions on the assumption that she was you. And I thought you were enormously ugly.

I should have had more faith in fate, of all things, I should have known that what was in store for me, was better, was blissfully better. Not worse.

When I arrived, I was greeted by worse. And then you walk in the door.

Now what are we to do but marry?

RASHEEDA. Okay, let me clarify something. You are not that young.

You are not bad looking, it's true, but this will fade, I am not a romantic like my mother was. Every man she loved she carried him in her body. In her arms, in her legs, in her feet.

In the end she was bent over carrying a lot of dead men in her body. I prefer the life of the mind.

And then, you killed my mother. She was not that nice to me, but she was my mother. So, this is not in your favour.

Lastly,

I am engaged.

SIMON. You're busy?

RASHEEDA. Engaged to be married. My fiancé.

He's a lawyer. He's attractive.

He's very talented. Can sing, play the guitar, has an excellent eye for composition.

He sees me aesthetically when he looks at me, I can tell by the look in his eye that he is framing me to my benefit. This makes me very happy, he will never look at me wrongly. I am even considering wearing sweatpants...

SIMON. Rasheeda.

RASHEEDA. Considering.

SIMON. But you can't marry him.

RASHEEDA. Why?

SIMON. It's not love.

RASHEEDA. Love is like dirt, like sweaty hair, like scarves with no perfume on them, like the shoes of men who are not your father piled up at the door, like the feet of men who are not your father sticking out from under the bedsheets, like the head of the man who is not your father hiding underneath the pillow...

I prefer marriage.

SIMON. It could, it can be the same thing.

RASHEEDA. No it can't.

SIMON. I am your betrothed Rasheeda I know! All my life I've been yours!

Please be reasonable!

RASHEEDA. I operate solely from reason.

Reason is my friend, my ally, my guardian.

It has protected me from bad nights with bad men. It has protected me from sun cancer.

And most importantly, it has protected me from believing that anybody else could tell me my fate.

SIMON. At your mother's funeral yesterday, I looked out into the hills and I realized how I had come to have certain expectations from my life. My wife lived only in my thoughts. She had habits. She didn't like to get sand in her shoes. She didn't like to think about snow because it made her feel cold. She could sing ancient songs.

RASHEEDA. I don't know any ancient songs.

SIMON. What will you do Rasheeda when you are old and my face flashes through your mind?

This face...look at it, this handsome, mobile face, full of lively expressiveness and dare I say it, affection-classic, unadulterated?

RASHEEDA. And what you speak of is regret. A small emotion.

Comparable to annoyance.

I don't know your name.

SIMON. Simon.

Son of Simon.

RASHEEDA. Why did your father call you after himself?

SIMON. Actually, his name was Solomon. But people here seem to have forgotten so I've kept up the pretense.

RASHEEDA. Well, you too have a way with pretense don't you, Simon son of Solomon? I have no patience with this.

Fiction is for the weak.

On the subject, the rather delicate subject of your willful assassination of my aged mother, I will not be pressing charges.

I'm willing to let the whole thing go.

For a small sum.

Which shall be decided on my meeting with my accountant in the morning.

SIMON. Rasheeda.

I have flown all this way.

On a plane.

With hard edges and soft seats.

I stand before you after decades of waiting, of yearning to wear the shoes of my father. I can't change what's already written for me. And that is you.

Please. Consider it. For my sake.

RASHEEDA. Who taught you to speak like that...?

      (The sound of a plane overhead. She thinks.)

Is it cold where you live?

SIMON. In winter...yes in winter it's cold.

RASHEEDA. I like the cold.

      (She turns and goes away. She shuts the door.)

Father My Friend

Wednesday Morning

*(A cock crows. **SIMON** and the **PRIEST** meet by Anna Cecilia Rasheeda's grave. The **PRIEST** smokes, wears sunglasses and looks through his binoculars.)*

SIMON. Are those the high school girls swimming Father?

PRIEST. I'm looking at the birds above their heads.

(Sighs.)

A little more to the left...there...that's it.

SIMON. You do this in public?

PRIEST. I'm going through a few things.

SIMON. Father...

PRIEST. What?

SIMON. How did you realize this was your calling?

PRIEST. I heard a loud voice. It came rolling down as though from the heavens.

I looked up to see my father over my head with an empty bottle of scotch and a rolling pin.

He wanted me to enter a secure profession.

SIMON. Good pay?

PRIEST. Terrible. But regular.

SIMON. And the calling?

PRIEST. He stopped when I stopped sending him money. He calls my brother now.

I know because I only live down the street and I can hear them trading curses over the clothesline.

SIMON. I meant...your calling?

PRIEST. Oh.

Oh, *He* never called.

I'm still waiting by the phone.

Which is hard because...we don't have one yet. But I'm getting wireless did I tell you?

SIMON. That's terrific.

PRIEST. My sister's paying for it, she's a sweetheart.

SIMON. If I hadn't been "called", I'd never have come.

PRIEST. You would have come. You were betrothed. They all come.

SIMON. I killed her.

PRIEST. We've been through this Simon, you're not responsible.

SIMON. I am.

I killed her.

PRIEST. Come here, let me hug you.

(They hug.)

SIMON. Father, thank you for holding me.

PRIEST. You're very welcome.

SIMON. Father.

PRIEST. What is it, son?

SIMON. Do you prefer men to women?

PRIEST. ...

All God's children are equal in my eyes.

SIMON. Oh.

...Father?

PRIEST. What?

SIMON. If I were to get married again, would you do the honors?

PRIEST. Of course! In five, ten years when you feel you are ready?

SIMON. How about tomorrow?

PRIEST. ...

OK, I'll do it.

Sons and Lovers

Wednesday Evening

*(The bench. **SOLOMON** and **GONAN** play cards. **SIMON** stands looking on.)*

SOLOMON. Rasheeda? You can't.

SIMON. Why not?

SOLOMON. You can't just marry, anyone.

SIMON. She's not anyone. She's a model.

SOLOMON. Find someone else.

Did you look by the donkey shed like I told you? See anything you like?

SIMON. But you chose her for me.

SOLOMON. You can't marry her.

SIMON. Why?

Why, is she my sister???

SOLOMON. God no.

SIMON. Is it because you're still having an affair with her mother?

*(**GONAN** puts his head in his hands.)*

It's true, isn't it?

SOLOMON. He's my best friend so he won't mind me, will you Gonan?

*(**GONAN** gestures as if to say "go ahead".)*

Let me tell you something, affairs are like cosmic explosions of the senses. They keep all your parts in working order. She did her duty, your mother. But the affair, it kept me alive...

SIMON. And now you're dead you're still seeing the woman.

SOLOMON. Your mother and I were not betrothed at birth.

Then I discovered I had a, you could say, calling to be with more than one woman. And Gonan's wife, Cecilia, you could say had a calling to be with me.

SIMON. And what about Maria? What about my mother?

SOLOMON. In that cosmos of exploded senses, your mother was a black hole. I got sucked in, ha ha right Gonan! Literally.

SIMON. That's disgusting.

SOLOMON. Look. Look at Gonan.

Sitting here with mud on his shoes.

You get mud in your shoes you get stuck.

GONAN. ...

SIMON. What does that mean?

SOLOMON. Just like his mother. Deaf as a fish.

What does he want? What do you want?

SIMON. I'm here to tell you. I'm doing it. I'm marrying her.

SOLOMON. You can't!

SIMON. Why not?

SOLOMON. I told you I'm banging the mother!

SIMON. Why didn't you think of this BEFORE you betrothed me?

I never get what I want! Even when you choose for me, I only ever do what you think I can do! Which is nothing! I lost my betrothed. She was dead when I arrived. And then she was alive and then she died and then she came back and I'm not going to let her go again. She's mine. You said so!

SOLOMON. Marry Rasheeda you'll be cursed!

SIMON. What?

What're you going to do?

SOLOMON. I can't do anything. It's just the way it is. I made mistakes.

And I didn't pay for them.

SIMON. I'm not making a mistake.

SOLOMON. We all make mistakes, bad mistakes we can't take back!

What are you looking at him for Gonan, you think he's got a flush up his ass?

SIMON. How much longer can you take this Gonan?

SOLOMON. He has to take it.

SIMON. Why?

SOLOMON. ...

GONAN. ...

SOLOMON. Stay away from the girl because, hey, look at me. Look at me.

I'm in heaven playing cards.

And so this is the way it works. The sins of the Father...

SIMON. The sins of the Father what?

I can afford to pay for your sins!

SOLOMON. Doesn't listen. Just like his mother. Gonan, this man is not my son.

GONAN. ...

SIMON. I'm marrying her Dad.

SOLOMON. Stay away from her. I'm warning you.

SIMON. You can't stop me.

SOLOMON. That's what you think. She's a woman.
She won't keep.

Marrying the One You Love

Thursday Morning

(The wedding: The **PRIEST** *marries* **SIMON** *and* **RASHEEDA** *at the grave of Anna Cecilia.)*

PRIEST. Dearly beloved, we are gathered here, to join this man and this woman...

SIMON. You can skip that part.

PRIEST. OK. Do you agree?

RASHEEDA. I checked with my accountant.

PRIEST. Do you agree?

SIMON. My lawyer says it's fine.

RASHEEDA. We leave for Pittsburgh as soon as I get my passport?

SIMON. The very second Rasheeda.

RASHEEDA. The Ural Mountains will no longer be my boundary.

PRIEST. To have and to hold.

Till death do you part.

> *(***RASHEEDA*** *takes a ring from* **SIMON**. *She looks at it. It looks familiar. She shrugs and puts it on her finger.)*

SIMON. Not even death will part us.

I'm sure of that now.

RASHEEDA. Kiss me.

(He does.)

We are going to be very happy.

And so is the baby.

(She leaves.)

SIMON. The what?

(**RASHEEDA** *steps outside.*)

[RASHEEDA'S SONG: "MY MOTHER, MYSELF"]

RASHEEDA.
CLIMB THE HIGHEST HILL I CAN,
SWEEP MY EYES OVERLAND.
I LOOK TO THE CLOUDS,
WHAT DO I FEEL?
A WOMAN PLEASED TO BE HERSELF?
A WOMAN PLEASED TO SEE HERSELF?
CLIMB THE TALLEST TREE I CAN,
SEE THE WORLD FROM WHERE I AM.
I LOOK TO THE CLOUDS,
WHAT DO I FEEL?
A WOMAN PLEASED TO BE HERSELF?
A WOMAN PLEASED TO SEE HERSELF?
NO! I FEEL MY MOTHER.
OH! I FEEL MY MOTHER.
FLOATING IN THE SKY AND THE SEA.
WHEN I'M TRYING TO BE ME.

I GO TO MY LOVER'S BED.
HOLD MY HANDS TO HIS HEAD.
HE'S NOT LIKE ANYONE ELSE
I'M NOT LIKE ANYONE ELSE.
NOTHING LIKE OUR MOTHERS!
ORIGINAL TO EACH OTHER.
BUT WHEN HE LOOKS AT ME.
WHAT DOES HE SEE?
YES!
HE SEES MY MOTHER
OH! HE SEES MY MOTHER.

RASHEEDA.

> FLOATING IN THE SKY AND THE SEA
> WHEN HE'S TRYING TO SEE ME.
>
> WHEN THE MIRROR'S BROKEN.
> WHEN MY HEART IS BROKEN.
> I CAN'T BE PLEASED TO SEE MYSELF.
> I CAN'T BE PLEASED TO BE MYSELF.
> I LOOK IN THE MIRROR!
> I LOOK IN THE MIRROR!
> WHAT DO I SEE?
> I SEE HER FACE,
> INSIDE OF ME.
> SO, I CAN NEVER ... BE FREE.

Seduction of the Mouth II

Thursday Night

*(Rasheeda's wedding dress is laid to waste, in haste. Now there's an old laptop computer in the space. Half-light. **RASHEEDA** and **SIMON** in bed. They try.)*

SIMON. That was wonderful…really! You're terrific Rasheeda…

Everything is just how it should be.

RASHEEDA. *(Deadpan.)* Are we finished?

SIMON. I… I think so…?

RASHEEDA. Good.

Good night.

SIMON. Rasheeda…?

RASHEEDA. Yes.

SIMON. Do you think we should get some kind of help?

RASHEEDA. My mother always brought the animals to bed with her. She said it livened things up.

SIMON. No.

I don't think the cows would fit.

RASHEEDA. Suit yourself Simon.

SIMON. Would you…would you like to play a game Rasheeda?

RASHEEDA. I hate games.

SIMON. No no, like a, a fun game…we could. I could wear a sack for you.

RASHEEDA. A what?

SIMON. I don't know…

RASHEEDA. That's just weird.

(*A noise outside.*)

SIMON. Wait...what was that?

RASHEEDA. What?

SIMON. Did you hear that?

It sounded like a moo.

RASHEEDA. A moo... Oh...

Must be

Must be the...let me go see.

(**RASHEEDA** *tears out of bed.*)

SIMON. Rasheeda...

Where are you going?

RASHEEDA. Out.

SIMON. You're leaving?

RASHEEDA. For a walk.

I don't know.

(*She leaves.*)

SIMON. What is wrong with her? Don't you care about me? Rasheeda?????

(*She walks out of the front door. We hear* **SOLOMON***'s muffled laughter.* **GONAN** *plays solitaire on his own.*)

(*Blackout.*)

Baby is Best

Friday Morning

(**RASHEEDA** *and* **SIMON** *peer into a crib.* **SIMON** *holds a toy aeroplane up and makes plane noises.)*

SIMON. He has everything he needs. Why doesn't he smile?

RASHEEDA. He's not interested in humor.

He's made the decision to side with reason over humor.

SIMON. He's a baby.

RASHEEDA. He's precocious.

He's a philosopher.

You can tell by the shape of his head.

It's conical.

He's a thinker.

SIMON. I'm depressed. I want my son to smile.

(**SIMON** *looks closely at the baby.)*

What's he doing?

Where did that come from?

RASHEEDA. Every baby needs toys.

SIMON. Are those cards?

Is he...shuffling?

RASHEEDA. Since yesterday.

With one hand.

SIMON. But he can barely breathe!

RASHEEDA. At least he's expressing himself.

In this unique way.

At least he's trying to be in this house in a good way.

SIMON. I could express myself to you Rasheeda.

Tell you how much I love you more?

RASHEEDA. Be a man Simon.

You have other parts to do the talking.

SIMON. Rasheeda...?

RASHEEDA. Yes.

SIMON. What will the baby do in Pittsburgh?

RASHEEDA. He wants to set up a gambling table.

For the over fifties.

He says that's where the market is.

SIMON. Oh?

RASHEEDA. He says the breast feeding is enjoyable.

But it's interrupting his smoking.

SIMON. We can't let him smoke Rasheeda! He'll die!

RASHEEDA. That's not a problem.

The baby is like me Simon.

He knows what he wants.

In Pittsburgh he will be the teacher.

Teaching them the cards.

He will be very happy.

His fruit will never wither.

Unlike some people's...

(*She leaves.*)

(**SIMON** *looks back in the crib.*)

SIMON. Are you looking at me sweetness?

Are you looking at me dear boy?

You're looking away...

Why are you looking away?

Oh god, he's ignoring me.

Don't ignore me.

Why are you ignoring me – they're only cards!

...

Dad...?

Is that you...? Dad???

DAD???!!!!

Bringing up Baby

Friday Evening

(**SIMON** *stands with the* **PRIEST** *at the grave of Anna Cecilia Rasheeda. The* **PRIEST** *now has long hair. He wears leather pants.)*

SIMON. I think my father is my son.

PRIEST. That's profound.

SIMON. Every time I pick him up, an ace falls out of his diapers.

PRIEST. I have...some other engagements to attend do my son. Why are we here again?

SIMON. Please, please support me Father.

Come and exorcise our son.

PRIEST. Why? Isn't he getting enough?

SIMON. Ex*or*cise. Get rid of my father inside him.

PRIEST. I can't do that.

I don't know how.

That stuff is quite...

It's outdated.

I wouldn't know where to begin.

But maybe it could be fun.

Like Ouija.

I used to play that.

We'd play it during pajama parties.

Me and the boys...so much fun.

SIMON. I think she's having an affair. I keep having these dreams of men coming in through the window. I dream that they leak in through the shutters.

PRIEST. I didn't think you believed in dreams.

SIMON. My father used to steal women from his brother's dreams.

She leaves the house all the time, goes in and out like a ghost.

Her mother never left.

You have to help me Father, I can't go on like this.

PRIEST. Who do you think she's youknowwhatting with?

SIMON. Somebody she's made up. They're the worst.

I'm scared he'll steal her from me.

PRIEST. You're scared of the invisible?

SIMON. The invisible is our greatest threat, Father.

PRIEST. I think I know what to do.

Come with me!

The Fountain of Knowledge

Friday Evening

(The **PRIEST** *sits on the bench.* **SIMON** *arrives with the old laptop computer.)*

SIMON. What are we going to do?

(The **PRIEST** *sits down with it and begins typing.)*

PRIEST. We are going to "Ask Jeeves".

We are going to "Ask Jeeves" "how to make one's betrothed fall in love with you".

SIMON. I don't think this is going to work.

PRIEST. Ye of little faith.

SIMON. What? What does it say?

PRIEST. Eye of newt blah blah blah.

(He scans.)

Ginger hair…my cousin's got some on his head.

I have everything else at home.

I mix everything. You drink. Don't smell, just drink.

It shouldn't take long to work. Happy?

SIMON. I can finally be with her in the way that was written in the sand, in my dreams…

PRIEST. And she with you. I'll send it to you this evening with instructions tied with a ribbon. A manly one so she won't suspect anything…like Burberry.

Tonight's going to be hot Simon, if you know what I mean…

Leave the windows open.

SIMON. We always do.

(**SIMON** *leaves.*)

PRIEST. Since I'm here…

(*He types solemnly.*)

I'm a lovely, sweet, lonely man, married to God.

Name: Father…that won't do.

Priestypriest243

Location: anywhere.

Education: doesn't matter.

Photograph: absolutely.

In my own words: what words are not my own?

Confused about most things, including life purpose.

Great clarity about most things, including life purpose.

Contradictory individual likes men and women.

Godloving, in a secular way.

Preferred match: Handsome/beautiful. Free thinking. Betrothed to no one else…

Betrothed? Who was I betrothed to? What about my betrothed? Scratch that, I like men and women who ARE my betrothed.

There's probably only one of you out there.

Find me.

(*He clicks "submit." He leaves.*)

To Make Your Betrothed Fall in Love With You

Friday Night

> *(**SIMON** stands semi-naked. He holds a vial in one hand and in the other he holds a clear plastic bag. The **PRIEST** stands just off and we hear his voice reading instructions.)*

PRIEST. To make your betrothed fall in love with you.

You have to awake in her the fire of a beloved for a beloved.

To walk the path of life and death with you.

Death the opposite of life.

You have to cherish her.

You have to kiss her feet.

You have to raise her to the stars.

Listen to the dance her heart makes.

Touch the strength in the soles of her feet, the arch of her back…

To make your betrothed fall in love with you,

You have to put five hundred dollars (American) into a small plastic bag.

Into the same bag, you must put your passport.

> *(**SIMON** puts his passport and the money into the bag.)*

Once you have done this, you have to drink this liquid mixed from the fire of a lamb's shank, and the ginger hair from my cousin's head. Don't smell. Just drink.

You have to now take off your clothes.

If you have done this already you are ahead of me.

(**SIMON** *gulps the mixture from the vial.*)

Now you are ready.

To dance…like a dirty dancer.

> *(The music starts up. An American pop anthem through the filter of an Eastern European folk song*. **SIMON** dances. It starts small and then builds in intensity. Until he's dancing for his life, his love. His trance-like dance escalates into a wild crescendo where we believe he has broken the boundary between life and death; between himself and his love.)*
>
> *(The door blows open.)*
>
> (**SIMON** *closes his eyes tight for the surprise. He opens them, and spins around. A silhouette of a young woman with a suitcase at the door.)*
>
> *(Blackout.)*

---

* A license to produce *The Betrothed* does not include a performance license for any third-party or copyrighted music. Licensees should create an original composition or use music in the public domain. For further information, please see Music Use Note on page iii.

Playing for Both Teams

Saturday Morning

(**RASHEEDA** *and* **SIMON** *in bed. Post coitus.*
Half-light.)

SIMON. *(Breathless.)* Rasheeda...

When I saw you come in the door –

RASHEEDA. Uh huh.

SIMON. I didn't think so.

RASHEEDA. That's your problem Simon, you don't think.

My passport came and I wanted to inform you, but you
were naked.

SIMON. I was ready for you Rasheeda.

RASHEEDA. So, I thought, "OK, why not? I'm almost in
Pittsburgh."

SIMON. You didn't want to?

RASHEEDA. You could say that I didn't want to.

Oh well, time to pack.

(**SIMON** *takes* **RASHEEDA***'s hands.)*

SIMON. No wait, Rasheeda...did you feel that?

RASHEEDA. What?

SIMON. Oh my GOD!

RASHEEDA. Oh Simon...

SIMON. Every part of me, it's throbbing...just like an
aeroplane...

It's working! Hair of ginger hear my cry ohhhhh!

RASHEEDA. Wait...oh... OH?!

SIMON. You feel it too!!! MOOOOOOO!

RASHEEDA/CECILIA. Simon son of Simon…

SIMON. …

RASHEEDA/CECILIA. Would you like to put your face between my legs?

SIMON. Cecilia…is that you?

It's me, Simon!

RASHEEDA/CECILIA. I know!

>*(Lights rise.* **RASHEEDA/CECILIA** *pulls away from him.)*

SIMON. You're my betrothed.

CECILIA. I've always been your betrothed. I tried to tell you!

SIMON. Is it really you in that body?

CECILIA. Yes!

SIMON. Inside…your sagging breasts and grey hair?

CECILIA. Yes, Simon! It's really me!

SIMON. How do we get you out?

CECILIA. If you want me, you have to kill this body.

That will release me.

SIMON. Why? You're perfect now.

Just stay.

CECILIA. I can't stay in this body Simon.

It's too weak for me.

It's not fucking beautiful enough.

SIMON. Beg to differ.

CECILIA. What do you see Simon?

SIMON. I don't know! Is it really you in there?

CECILIA. Yes, yes, it's me, I'm a hag inside I promise!

SIMON. So where is she? Where's Rasheeda?

(A loud banging.)

CECILIA. She's in the broom closet. In a mouse.

SIMON. How did you get here?

CECILIA. You called me. I heard.

When the betrothed calls.

We come. We all come.

SIMON. I can't kill you.

CECILIA. Why? You killed me once. Do it again.

SIMON. No.

CECILIA. Kill me.

SIMON. I can't do it.

CECILIA. KILL ME!

SIMON. But you look young!

CECILIA. What, you can't kill me in this body?

SIMON. I'm no saint, Cecilia. But I was taught never to raise a hand to a woman.

CECILIA. But an old woman...

SIMON. No one said anything about old women!

CECILIA. Look around Simon.

Your wife doesn't love you.

Your dead father is fucking her.

He is also sitting inside your son when he can't have her so he can watch you suffer.

SIMON. I've seen it in his eyes, the way he looks at me when I'm on the toilet.

CECILIA. He can never stay long, but he's watching.

SIMON. Where will you go when I kill you?

CECILIA. There's no saying Simon.

I could be a plant.

Or a reptile.

Or a cow.

Or a beautiful woman.

Or...

SIMON. Or?

CECILIA. An old woman.

But I will always, always be your betrothed.

Do you want me?

SIMON. Yes.

CECILIA. Do you want me Simon son of Simon?

SIMON. YES!

CECILIA. Kill me now!

SIMON. NO!

CECILIA. I hate to think of snow because I get cold.

I don't like to get sand in my shoes.

I have a very pure desire for you.

It's worth it.

(**CECILIA** *takes* **SIMON**'*s hands.*)

Look at me, Simon son of Simon.

What do you see?

SIMON. I see...a heart good and pure.

A lap soft and sweet.

I see you Cecilia.

Just as you were.

I don't want Rasheeda...

I want you, holy woman.

CECILIA. Once you give your word to a woman.

Dead or alive. There's no going back.

Especially if you were

SIMON.	**CECILIA**.
Betrothed.	Betrothed.

SIMON. I give you my word Cecilia.

I want your sagging breasts and grey hair.

I'm going to do it.

I'm going to kill you.

Again.

CECILIA. AGAIN!

SIMON. AGAIN!

> *(He drags her to the door. He grabs a sack from under their bed. More banging.)*

Fuck you, Rasheeda!

CECILIA. Don't talk like that.

She's still my daughter.

SIMON. I love you Anna Cecilia Rasheeda Silosa Hangi Maria.

CECILIA. You know my name.

(They kiss gently.)

*(The banging gets louder. **SIMON** puts the sack over her head. She stands. He reaches for her and squeezes her neck tightly. She falls to the ground.)*

(He waits.)

(He waits.)

(He waits.)

(He waits.)

(Nothing.)

(Fade to black.)

Fathers

Saturday Afternoon

> (**SOLOMON** *and* **GONAN** *play cards. They look up when* **SIMON** *enters. Then, continue playing.)*

SIMON. Where is she?

SOLOMON. Dealer's pack Gonan, I'll cut.

SIMON. I want her.

SOLOMON. Like you want a limp dick.

> (**SIMON** *marches up to them and grabs the cards.* **SOLOMON** *stands.)*

Women are not possessions.

SIMON. What did you do with her?

SOLOMON. I warned you but you married her anyway and now you have her, all to yourself.

SIMON. You can keep my wife. I want my betrothed.

SOLOMON. Now whatever does he mean, Gonan?

Do I look like a thief? Stealing off in the middle of the night with someone else's property? If she was property, which she isn't.

SIMON. Rasheeda's a bucket of reason.

Her face makes me weep.

I don't miss her when she's not in our bed.

And frankly, neither should you.

You can keep her.

Just give me back my betrothed.

And get the hell out of my son.

I don't like you looking at me when I'm taking a bath.

Or when I'm on the toilet.

Or when I'm lying in bed, wishing I was somewhere else.

SOLOMON. You son's got colic.

SIMON. I want my betrothed.

SOLOMON. Oh, the one you killed? If you care so much about her, why did you kill her?

SIMON. Just give her back.

SOLOMON. I'm not God. I don't know where she is.

SIMON. Rasheeda's body is in my bed, but Cecilia's gone.

Where is she?

SOLOMON. She's not here anymore you sonofacow!

Cecilia left me.

They all leave.

SIMON. Cecilia left you? Then she isn't here?!

Where is she? Tell me!

SOLOMON. Make me.

(**SIMON** *leaps at* **SOLOMON** *and tackles him.*)

SIMON. You're not my father!

SOLOMON. Yes, I am!

SIMON. You love me!

SOLOMON. No, I don't!

SIMON. Yes, you do or else you wouldn't try so hard to get my attention.

(**SIMON** *gets* **SOLOMON** *in a headlock.*)

You love me!

SOLOMON. You little shit!

SIMON. No one cares about me the way you do.

You loved me so much you let me go.

You left Ma but you never left me!

SOLOMON. Your mother left me.

Maria left me.

For him!

> (**SOLOMON** *breaks. He weeps.* **SIMON** *holds* **SOLOMON** *in his arms.*)

They all leave.

GONAN. *(In a voice that hasn't seen the light in years.)* I know where she is.

SOLOMON. Gonan!

GONAN. Do you want her?

SIMON. Yes!

GONAN. But she's a woman. They don't keep.

SIMON. Tell me where she is!

GONAN. I know where she is. You haven't got long. Go!

> (**SIMON** *runs out.* **SOLOMON** *looks at* **GONAN**.)

SOLOMON. Thief.

GONAN. I didn't love her.

She came to me.

Then she left.

> (**SOLOMON** *leaves.*)

My friend...

*(**GONAN** sits on the bench exhausted. He notices the computer for the first time.)*

(He opens it.)

(He types as he speaks.)

I am Gonan.

Hobbies and Interests: Cards and Friends.

Employment: Sometimes.

In your own words: What words are not my own?

I was married once. I have depression and fibromyalgia. I used to be scared of the internet, but not any more.

Nowadays I am single and looking for a secular God-loving individual-type person who is liberal, contradictory, sweet.

(He looks up.)

Only respond if you are my betrothed. There is probably only one of you.

Post.

*(The computer pings. **GONAN**'s face lights up. He reads.)*

Priestypriest243.

Kinky.

Fathers II

Sunday Afternoon

(**SIMON** *sits beside* **GONAN** *in his house. The windows are closed. A mouse pedals rapidly on a little mouse wheel in the old mouse cage. They play cards in silence.*)

GONAN. Gin.

SIMON. I'm not good at this.

GONAN. No.

SIMON. You miss him?

GONAN. I like to win too.

SIMON. I'm not any good at this.

Gonan, I'm so sorry. For everything.

GONAN. Your father was like my brother.

You are like my son. I don't remember my girl so well.

Strange, huh?

Don't be sorry for yourself. Be true. Be sad for your son.

SIMON. What's it like being dead?

GONAN. ...

I'm still stuck Simon.

I beat you again.

You're a good loser.

SIMON. Gonan. She never came.

And my son...what's inside my son?

GONAN. It's you.

(They play in silence.)

*(**SIMON**'s son **CECIL** walks in. He's a young man in his late teens.)*

*(He sits with **GONAN** and **SIMON**. **SIMON** leans over and ruffles the boy's hair.)*

(The men widen the circle and deal for three.)

(The window blows open.)

(We hear a woman laughing.)

(Stage grows dark.)

The Journey II

Sunday Evening

(**CECILIA** *sits in an aeroplane seat. She holds her age in every limb, in every pore of her body, in every crease of her face, every strand of her hair. It's as though time folded in on itself.)*

(She clutches a small transparent bag with Simon's money and passport. She counts the money and smiles.)

CECILIA. Back to the old cow country... Pittsburgh.

(She turns to the [absent] woman next to her.)

I love it when people next to you talk to you on the plane, ask you where you're going, what you're doing? It's a great way to make friends. I'm going to Pittsburgh. I'm going to teach English. In my country, I had only one pupil. He couldn't speak English at all until he met me, but he learned quick.

I can just see them...a big classroom full of students, boys and girls with their hands up in the air, full of questions, no answers. You age and age and never any answers...is it cold in America? I had one pupil. He was beautiful.

He gets cold when he thinks of snow.

He hates sand in his shoes.

He's beautiful.

I think I will like the cold...

(She pulls the blanket higher on her body.)

(The sound of an aeroplane taking off; its shadow crosses slowly over her body. She releases the shadow consciously through her left hand and watches as it floats all the way across the stage...until its arc is all we can see.)

End of Play

www.ingramcontent.com/pod-product-compliance
Lightning Source LLC
Chambersburg PA
CBHW070353120726
47909CB00008B/2830